HEY, LOOK AT ME!

I CAN HELP

Merry Fleming Thomasson

Illustrated by Charles Hogarth

I can help each day, you see.
Turn the page and look at me.

MERRYBOOKS & MORE • CHARLOTTESVILLE, VIRGINIA

Look at me getting up in the morning. I can help my parents when I dress myself. I can help the earth when I dress warmly for cold weather so we do not have to keep the house so warm and use more fuel.

EARTH FACT: Most of the energy we use at home is for heating and cooling, and about half of that is wasted.

Look at me eating my breakfast. I can help myself when I eat healthy foods like fresh fruit, lots of milk, and cereal. I can help the earth by thinking about what I need before I open the refrigerator, taking the food out quickly, and closing the door right away to save electricity.

EARTH FACT: We open our refrigerator more than 20 times a day. That is more than 7,000 times a year.

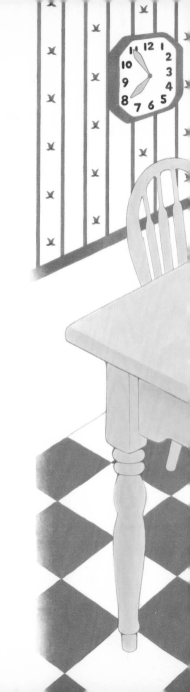

Look at me learning in school. I can help my teacher by listening and not talking out of turn. I can help the earth by learning about plants and animals, and what I can do to protect them.

EARTH FACT: About 1,000 kinds of animals and plants become extinct every year. That means, like the dinosaurs, they disappear from the earth forever.

Look at me having fun in school. I can help my friends by sharing crayons, toys, and books with them. I can help the earth by reusing all my lunch containers and collecting aluminum cans and bottles. This is called recycling.

EARTH FACT: We throw out around 26 billion jars and bottles a year that could be recycled. We use 2.5 million plastic bottles every hour; many of them cannot be recycled.

Look at me playing outside in the fresh air and sunshine. I can help myself by running and riding my bike to keep my body strong and healthy. I can help the earth by picking up litter wherever I see it.

EARTH FACT: It takes an aluminum can lying on the ground over 200 years to disappear.

Look at me with my animal friends. I can help my parents by learning to feed my pets. I can help the earth by feeding the ducks and rabbits and other animals that live in my neighborhood. I can also help by planting trees and shrubs to provide them shelter or a home.

EARTH FACT: The average person uses more than six trees a year in paper, wood, and other products made from trees.

Look at me taking a bath.
I can help my parents by
bathing myself and
brushing my teeth. I can
help the earth by using
less water when I bathe and
brush my teeth, and by
making sure the faucet
doesn't leak.

EARTH FACT: A leaky faucet can waste
enough water in a year to fill 60 bathtubs.

Look at me talking and reading with my father. I can help myself by looking at books and listening to my parents read to me. I can help the earth by bundling up the newspapers and recycling them when my parents are finished reading them.

EARTH FACT: We would save 500,000 trees every week, if we recycled our Sunday newspapers.

Look at me going to bed. I can
help my parents by getting
myself ready for bed,
getting my clothes out for
the next day, and putting
everything away. I can help
the earth by thinking about the
things I can do every day. I can
save water and electricity. I can
recycle. I can be nice to the
animals and plants and keep
our neighborhood clean.

EARTH FACT: There is only one earth and we
each need to do our part to save it.

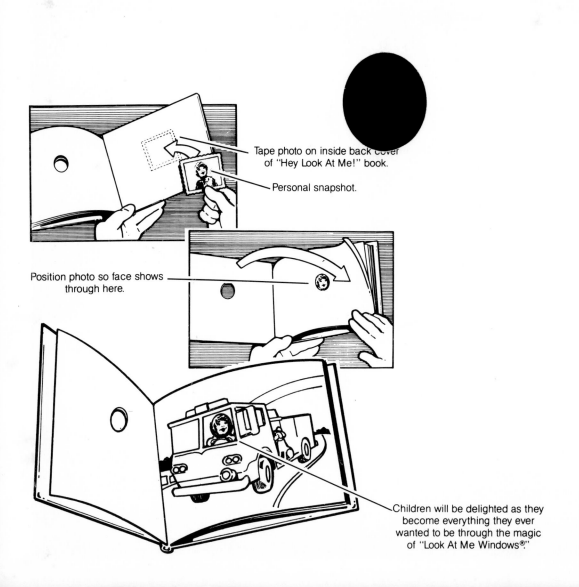

Tape photo on inside back cover of "Hey Look At Me!" book.

Personal snapshot.

Position photo so face shows through here.

Children will be delighted as they become everything they ever wanted to be through the magic of "Look At Me Windows®."